Printer's Devil Court

Printer's Devil Court

SUSAN HILL

P

PROFILE BOOKS

First published in Great Britain in 2014 by
PROFILE BOOKS LTD
3A Exmouth House
Pine Street
London ECIR OJH
www.profilebooks.com

1 3 5 7 9 10 8 6 4 2

Typeset in Fournier by MacGuru Ltd
info@macguru.org.uk

Printed and bound in Great Britain by
Clays, Bungay, Suffolk

The moral right of the author has been asserted.

A CIP catalogue record for this book is
available from the British Library.

ISBN 978 1 78125 365 6
eISBN 978 1 78283 114 3

Inner Temple
Library

Temple, Farley and Freeman. Solicitors
2 Delvers Court
St James's SW1

Dear Sir

The enclosed item has been sent on to me by
Messrs. Geo Rickwell, Antiquarian Book-
seller, with the instruction that it be passed
on to the beneficiaries of the estate of the late
Dr Hugh Meredith. As you know, the library
in which it was found was entrusted for sale
to Messrs Rickwell. Of a few items not in-
cluded in the sale, mainly for reasons of poor
physical condition, the enclosed was deemed
to have no commercial value. I am therefore
sending it to you to deal with in any way you
see fit. I would be grateful for acknowledge-
ment of its receipt in due course,

Yours etc.

The book in question measures some eight inches square and the sheets, of a pleasing cream paper, had been folded and hand-sewn together with heavy card backing – a neat and careful piece of amateur book-binding. Apparently this, together with botanical illustration and embroidery, was one of the soothing hobbies taken up by Dr Meredith in old age, when he had long ceased practice medicine, not only because of his advancing years, the family story has it, but because he suffered from sort of intermittent nervous condition.

The book has no title on the cover or the spine but on the first page is written

The Wrong Life.

Hugh Meredith MD

The Book

In my first year as a junior doctor I moved into lodgings in a small court close by Fleet Street, an area which could not at the time have changed greatly since the days of Dickens. The court was small and the tall, narrow, grimy houses faced into a dismal yard, at one end of which a passageway led into the main thoroughfare. At the other end, a similar snicket led to the graveyard and thence to the church of St Luke-by-the-Gate. The church was pressed in on either side by two warehouse buildings and most of the graveyard was ancient and no longer in use. Old stones leaned this way and that, monuments and tombs were greened and yellowed over with moss and lichen. One or two trees struggled upwards to find what little light they could, and at their bases, more gravestones, sunken flat to the earth, were almost entirely obscured by weeds, ivy and rank grasses. In between was a mulch of dead leaves. I sometimes took a short cut through the churchyard on my way – often late – to the hospital. Once, when my sister was visiting me and I took her that way, she said that she could not understand why I was not frightened out of my wits when walking.

'Frightened of what?'

'Ghosts … the dead.

'As to ghosts, my dear Clara, I do not believe in them for a moment and dead bodies I see in the hospital every day so why would either of those things frighten me? The only thing to be wary of in these dark hidden corners of London are living thieves and pickpockets. Even the vagrants can be threatening after they have been drinking illicit cider.' I laughed, as nevertheless, Sarah pulled me by the arm to hasten our way to the main gate.

When this story begins its late and dismal autumn. Every morning mist rose and hung over the river after a cold night and when it turned milder for a day or two, the choking fog rolled over the city, muffling sounds, blurring the outlines of buildings and tasting foul in the mouth and nostrils, so that everyone went about with their faces half-covered in mufflers. Braziers burned at the street corners, where the hot chestnut and potato sellers rubbed hands stiff and blue with cold. Traffic crawled along the Strand to Fleet Street, headlamps looming like great hazy moons out of the mist. Fleet Street was a din of hot metal presses turning out the daily and evening newspapers. Open a small wooden door in a wall and you saw down into a bedlam of huge iron machines and the clatter of chutes, down which rolled the *Evening News* and *Standard*, *The Times* and the *Chronicle*, by the mile. Men at work below were dwarfed by the presses, faces grimy with oil and the air was thick with the smell of it and of fresh ink and hot paper. I loved it and wandered these old streets whenever I had a half hour to spare, venturing up unfamiliar passages and alleys into Courts and Buildings, discovering hidden churches and little gardens. But best of all I liked to walk beside the river, or to stand on the terrace of the medical school which overlooked its great flowing expanse, now treacle black, now sparkling in the sun and carrying so many and various craft on its tide. Such idle moments were rare, however. I was usually attending patients, following great physicians on their ward rounds, learning from the surgeons in theatre and the pathologists in the mortuary. I loved my work as I had loved every moment of my studies. I suppose the latest in a line of doctors would either take to medicine as a duck to water or rebel and become a bank manager.

Two other doctors lived at number two, Printer's Devil Court, at the time of which I write. Walter Powell, a year ahead of the rest, James Kent and Rafe McAllister. James and I occupied one floor, Walter and Rafe the other. It was a dark house, with steep, narrow stairs and we each had a miserably small bedroom and shared bathroom, with temperamental plumbing.

But we had one large sitting room which stretched the width of the house and had a coal fire with a chimney that drew well, a reasonably comfortable sofa and three armchairs. There was a handsome mahogany table at which we ate and sometimes worked. The room had two windows, one at either end, in each of which stood a desk. There was precious little natural light and the outlook was of the opposite buildings. By now it was dark at 4 o'clock and lamps and fire were lit early. We kept irregular hours, sometimes working all day and all night, so that we only met to eat or relax together a couple of times a week. The landlady, Mrs Ratchet, rarely spoke a word but she looked after us well enough in her way, cleaning and clearing, making the beds and the fire and providing food at odd hours. We were fortunate, hard-working and innocent – or so I thought. I got on well with my fellows. James was a simple, easy-going man, with little imagination with a great deal of human sensibility. He was a plain-speaking and compassionate doctor in the making. Rafe was serious, studious and silent. He was never unfriendly and yet I could not get to know him – he presented a closed-off front and seemed to live in a world of test tubes and apparently dreamed only of finding cures for rare and obscure conditions. He had little to do with patients, which was probably for the best but I judged that one day he would make some remarkable medical breakthrough, in his own, intense and purposeful way.

Walter Power was an even more complex character. If ever I felt a dislike or approval of any of my fellows, it was of him. He was jovial and friendly enough but he had a sly way with him and something shadowy in his personality though I could not have put a finger on quite what – at least not then. The only way I can give any idea of how he – and indeed, Rafe – affected me is to say that I would happily have entrusted my life to James but to Walter and Rafe, never.

Part Two

I

It was a murky November evening with a fog off the river and a fuzzy halo round every street lamp, when the conversation which had such a hideous outcome took place. We had all four of us returned to our lodging house earlier than usual and eaten our lamb stew and treacle pudding together at the big table – Mrs Ratchet knew how to line the stomachs of hungry young doctors in such a bleak weather. Everything had been cleared away and we sat with the precious bottle of port, generously provided by James's wine merchant brother, around a good fire. James and Walter had lit their pipes and the sweet smell of Old Holborn tobacco was pleasing to the two of us who did not smoke.

We had begun to talk in an idle way about the day's work. I had been following an eminent thoracic specialist on his ward round, taking in as much as I could – he kept up a brisk pace – about rare lung diseases, and then working in the crowded outpatient clinics. Walter had been in the mortuary, assisting at the post mortems of bodies washed up or pulled out of the River Thames. One had been trapped under the hull of an abandoned barge several weeks, he told us with a certain relish. I shuddered but he merely smiled his tight little smile.

'You will have to acquire a stronger stomach for the game, Hugh.'

'Hardly a game.'

He shrugged and for a moment we all fell silent. The fire shifted down. James bent forward and threw on another couple of coals. And then Walter said, 'What opinions do we all have about the story of the raising of Lazarus?'

I suppose the leap from bodies drowned in the River Thames to the New Testament story of the man miraculously raised from the dead by Jesus, was not such a great one but the question silenced us again.

'I'm not sure I remember many of the details,' I said at last. 'I rather switched off the chapel sermons in my senior school years.'

James said that he knew the story. Rafe did not speak.

'Or that of the centurion's daughter?' Walter continued, taking the pipe from his mouth to smile again. I remember noticing what a pale complexion he had, even in the ruddy glow from the fire, which gave the others a more cheerful aspect. Walter's hair was already receding, showing his high forehead and oddly large skull.

'Come, you must all have some theory.'

'I am no biblical scholar,' James said, 'but for what it is worth, I believe fully in the stories. They have the ring of truth.'

'Of course,' Walter nodded. 'You, as a conscientious Christian would. But as a medical man?'

Rafe got up abruptly and went out. We heard his footsteps going up the stairs two at a time. He returned to the room carrying a Bible.

'Let us read the exact accounts before we express any further opinions.'

I noted that it took him almost no time to find the relevant pages, which surprised me as I had not put Rafe down as a religious man. We settled quietly while he read first, in two of the Gospels, the account of the raising of Jairus's daughter.

'Well, that seems quite straightforward,' James said. 'One line is conclusive and repeated in each gospel account. "The maid is not dead but sleepeth." As Jesus saw.'

'Yes, plenty of that sort of thing,' I said, 'we have all seen it – the deep coma resembling death. People have been pronounced dead and taken to the mortuary or even to the undertaker and consigned to their coffin, only to have woken again.'

'Perhaps that would take care of Luke, Chapter 7?'

Walter took up the Bible and, like Rafe,

found the page almost immediately.

'When he came to the gate of the city, behold, there was a dead man carried out … And Jesus came and touched the bier and said "Young man, I say to thee, arise. And he that was dead sat up and began to speak."'

'More problematic all the same. The man was on the bier being taken for burial, which has to take place very quickly in hot countries' Walter said. 'I vote that this was another case of the deep coma – the man had a lucky escape.'

James looked perturbed. Walter flipped the pages and found the story of the raising of Lazarus. 'Here,' he said, a slight smugness in his tone, 'this is unequivocal, I think.'

'Now he had been in the grave for four days …'

'Can we be sure of that ?' I asked.

'No, but the story is quite detailed – why would they lie? His sister says, "by this time he stinketh for he hath been dead four days."'

Rafe looked blank yet I thought I caught the glint of something like excitement in his eyes.

'Listen then, Walter continued, 'Jesus cried with a loud voice, "Lazarus, come forth." And he that was dead came forth, bound hand and foot with grave cloths and his face was bound about with a napkin.'

James sat back. 'And that,' he said, 'I do believe.'

Thinking to lighten the atmosphere, I knelt on the hearth rug and made up the fire, poking at it to loosen the ashes below, then adding more coals. The whole flared up so quickly that I started back and as I did so, I glanced round the room. James sat very still, his demeanour very calm. Rafe's face was closed and expressionless, his eyes down. Walter was looking directly at me with an expression I could not wholly read, but which seemed almost rapacious, so that I felt distinctly uncomfortable.

'I vote for another glass of port,' I said, 'if James would allow.'

He jumped up at once and busied himself over refilling the glasses. When he had seated himself again, Walter said, 'You two were not here when Rafe and I began discussions on this subject.'

'Discussion about the miracles of Jesus Christ?' I said, surprised.

'Not exactly,' Walter leaned forward and I caught the same glint in his eyes as I had noticed in Rafe's.'

'Oh, it was nothing but some macabre joking,' he said now, giving Walter a quick look, as if in warning. 'We had both had some encounters with death in its various forms that day and you know as well as I that we need a touch of gallows humour to see us through. That is why medical students traditionally play such ghoulish tricks on one another.'

James laughed. 'Like Anderson in the dissecting room and …'

Walter held out his hand. 'Yes, yes.' Something in his tone doused on mirth in the incident. 'But other than in those remote biblical times – and who knows how reliable the witnesses were after all? – Have any of us heard of men – or women, for that matter, being raised from the dead? By dead I mean exactly that. Dead.'

'Well of course not,' James said.

'Yet you are ready to believe in incidents recorded more than two thousand years ago.'

James nodded but said nothing.

'Let's leave biblical times. Do any of us believe that this miracle could be performed now? Though clearly not by the man Jesus.'

'So what are you talking about?' I asked. 'Do you mean by those who serve in His ministry now?'

'No. By men like us – doctors and scientists that we are.' I saw that he and Walter exchanged another glance.

'Is this some fantasy you have been beguiling yourselves with on your walks to and from the hospital?' I asked, for Walter and Rafe generally went together. Now, Rafe leaned forwards with some eagerness.

'It is far more than that, and we are not men to waste time on fantasies.'

James looked troubled but I simply laughed.

'Enough teasing,' I said, 'you had better tell us, as it's the time of a dismal evening for a good tale.' My voice sounded over-loud and hearty in the room.

'I assure you that I am deadly serious and so is Rafe. But if you cannot be, let us say no more on the subject.' Walter tamped and fidgeted away with his pipe.

'Come now,' I said, 'I will take you at your word. Let us hear what you have to say and we can make up our own minds.'

Walter continued to work away at the pipe, like an actor confident that he has his audience and can keep them waiting. Eventually it was linked to his satisfaction and he drew on it a few times before beginning.

'As you may have guessed by now, I have been considering our subject for some time. And because I am no more than a basic scientist, whereas Rafe here is a scientific genius, I have discussed it all with him. I have put difficult questions to him and he to me and we have each played devil's advocate. Now we have reached the point where we think we should bring you two into the secret. On one condition.'

He took the pipe from his mouth again and paused, enjoying the melodrama of the moment.

'So what is your condition, Walter?'

'That you must want to know, and know everything. If you do not – perhaps I will say "dare not" we will continue to share these agreeable lodgings with you both as usual and never mention the matter again.'

Walter looked steadfastly me and then James and I was so mesmerised by the look in his eyes as he stared that I could not glance away.

'That is all very well,' I said, 'but how on earth can I tell you I don't want to hear a word more when I don't know what it is all about?'

'But you do. You have been given more than a hint – quite enough on which to base a decision.'

'The subject being the miracles of raising the dead?'

'Not precisely. As I said, we are not biblical scholars and those times are long past. It was a convenient way of introducing the nature of the business, that is all.'

'Well for my part,' James said, 'I don't understand any of it.' He looked at me. 'I must say that my instincts tell me to remain in ignorance – even in innocence.'

I paused. I was still more or less convinced that the whole thing was an elaborate game on Walter's part. Rafe's chair was pulled back into the shadows so that his face was hidden, only his spectacles occasionally gleaming in the firelight. Now he said quietly, 'Just remember that what you know you can never unknow. If you are afraid …'

'Of course not. What trick could you to cook up that would be so alarming?'

Rafe did not reply.

'Make your decision,' Walter said.

'Before I reply,' I said, 'tell us why it is so important to make us party to whatever game you propose to play.'

'Because you may find it more interesting

23

and remarkable than you suppose. Because you will be entirely impartial witnesses. And because we may need your help. It would not be easy to find two other men we know so well and more importantly, whom we trust.'

'Is this enterprise dangerous?'

'To you? I am not sure. But I can see no reason why you would be at serious risk of harm.'

'Is it legal?'

'I have no idea. I suspect that the law has never been tested in the matter.'

Suddenly, my mind was made up. I slapped the arm of the chair. 'Then, dammit …'

But Walter held up his hand. 'Just one more thing, though I suspect I know what you have decided. If you are with us, you must swear solemnly that you will tell no one – no one. Now or at any time. If you are ever questioned, which is improbable, you must deny all knowledge or involvement.' His expression was as serious as a man's could be.

find him unloading what looked like half the contents of a laboratory and lugging it down the area steps. He certainly did not speak and I was feeling too rotten to ask any questions or offer him help.

The next time I saw him he was coming up from the basement, slipping a key into his pocket. He rarely joined us at supper now and when he did, he ate quickly and immediately made off downstairs. There were no more leisurely, companionable evenings when we four sat talking round the fire. Walter seemed to spend longer hours at the hospital, especially at night and when he was ᵇᵘ⁻ᵗ to his own room. Shortly after- ⁻ʳᵉᵗ episode

'Then I swear it,' I said, and as I did so, I felt an odd nervous lurch in my belly. 'I swear it and I am with you.'

Walter did not reply but turned to look at James, who had gone horribly pale.

'I cannot swear,' he said. 'I am not with you, whatever this nonsense is about and so I would rather not hear more.'

He got up quickly and nodding us good night, he left the room. We heard his footsteps and his door close. It was disconcerting. I liked and trusted James and for a moment, I thought of changing my mind. I looked at Walter and as I did so, I felt a flicker of alarm. Something in his eyes gave out a warning and a threat.

'Another glass of port,' I said hastily. 'I'm sure James would not object.'

Walter frowned. 'No, we need clear heads.'

I let the port stand but I tried to keep my tone light as I asked, 'Now – what is this all about? What are you proposing?'

'We are proposing,' Walter replied, 'to bring the dead back to life.'

2

I slept soundly that night perhaps becaus
I still believed that Walter's proposed experiment was nothing more than a jape.
first, nothing el

'Then I swear it,' I said, and as I did so, I felt an odd nervous lurch in my belly. 'I swear it and I am with you.'

Walter did not reply but turned to look at James, who had gone horribly pale.

'I cannot swear,' he said. 'I am not with you, whatever this nonsense is about and so I would rather not hear more.'

He got up quickly and nodding us good night, he left the room. We heard his footsteps and his door close. It was disconcerting. I liked and trusted James and for a moment, I thought of changing my mind. I looked at Walter and as I did so, I felt a flicker of alarm. Something in his eyes gave out a warning and a threat.

'Another glass of port,' I said hastily. 'I'm sure James would not object.'

Walter frowned. 'No, we need clear heads.'

I let the port stand but I tried to keep my tone light as I asked, 'Now – what is this all about? What are you proposing?'

'We are proposing,' Walter replied, 'to bring the dead back to life.'

Christmas came and went and we saw in the New Year merrily. I was preparing to return to London when on 2 January I received a telegram from Walter.

Enterprise critical stage.
Urgent you return and witness.

After the fogs and damp of late autumn, London had come in for one of the worst winters for decades. Snow had fallen thickly for several days and then frozen hard to the ground every night. Temperatures remained below freezing and twice plummeted to depths barely known since the Great Frost, when the Thames had frozen over.

The fire made little impression on the air of the sitting room and our windows were ferned and feathered over with ice, on the inside. The hospital, of course, was full to bursting point: vagrants and beggars died on the streets in shameful numbers and we were all working round the clock. I had hurried back as requested but for over two weeks Walter had no time to talk to me and Rafe was unable to work in his cellar laboratory, the cold was so intense. James I almost never saw and when I did, I felt that he had withdrawn from me as well as from the others and was wary of conversation.

On a night in early March when at last the thermometer hovered just above freezing, Walter knocked on my door well after one o'clock in the morning. He was wearing his outdoor clothes and there was something almost akin to an electrical charge about him, so that I jumped up from my desk in alarm.

'What has happened?'

'Nothing yet. But it is time. Come – Rafe is waiting.'

'Where are we going?'

'To the hospital. But we must go stealthily and take great care.'

The pavements were treacherous and piles of dirty, frozen snow lay in the gutters. The half-moon was hazy, so that we had to watch our every step and a raw and bitter wind blowing off the river scoured our faces.

The lamps at the hospital entrance gates glowed out but much of the building was dimmed, as people slept. We entered by the front doors and at once turned along a covered way to the old East Wing and then down three flights of stairs that led to the basement corridors. Walter's footsteps made barely a sound and I thought that he must have walked this way at night many times before. Once or twice he stopped, raised his hand, and listened, before continuing. I followed in his footsteps, barely able to breathe, I was so tense. We turned a corner into a short passageway with an unmarked double-door at the end. No one else was about. This part of the hospital was little used, though the old wards had been hastily re-commissioned to cope with the overflow of patients. The whole place smelled cold and slightly damp. We stopped and Walter tapped on the door, though not on the panel but on the frame, presumably so that the sound was muffled. At once, it was opened by Rafe. He so rarely gave anything away on his impassive features but now he wore an expression of scarcely concealed excitement and I felt the same strange electrical charge coming off him as I had noticed with Walter.

The second we were both inside, Rafe turned the key in the lock. The two did not speak as they moved into the centre of the small room. It was windowless, save for a row of rectangular panes high up along one side, and the walls were tiled to the ceiling. Two lamps stood on a laboratory bench, only one of which was lit and that dimly but it was enough for me to see about me.

Next to the lamps stood a small array of laboratory paraphernalia – test tubes, rubber piping, glass phials. A bunsen burner gave out a low, steady blue flame and there were a couple of items of medical equipment. In the body of the room stood a hospital trolley, levered to its full height and with the metal sides raised. On it was a still figure covered in a single grey blanket. I went closer, and saw that it was the body of an old man. His head was covered in grey stubble, with the same forming a close beard. His skin was bruise coloured and grime enseamed the neck, the skin below his eyes, and around the nose and ears. Clearly, though he looked to have been given a cursory wash, the dirt was ingrained so as to have become almost a part of the scheme itself. One hand was uncovered, the nails had recently been cut but more dirt was wedged beneath them and in the creases of the fingers.

At first glance, I took this to be a corpse but then I saw the faintest of movements as the breath rose and fell in the man's chest. Walter bent down and put a finger under the nostrils and nodded. The man's breathing was laboured and as we stood looking at him a rattle came from his throat. Walter glanced at Rafe and it was as if a flint has been struck and the quick spark passed between them.

'Yes,' Walter said, 'not long. A moment or two only but the old ones put up a brave fight. Life has been hard to them and they are used to battling.'

I started to say something but at first my

voice refused to come out and I could only make a hoarse croaking sound, as if it was I and not the old man fighting for breath. But eventually, I managed to speak.

'Who is he?'

Walter shrugged. 'Brought in from the street a couple of nights ago, half frozen to death and full of pneumonia. He had nothing on him but his clothes. His pockets were full of chestnut husks – he had probably been living off the scraps of nuts that fell onto the pavement and perhaps tossed a whole one now and again by the seller.'

'No name?'

'No name, no home, no family, no friends, no hope. He is not long for this world and will be better out of it.'

I had an uprush of terror as he said it, and took a quick step nearer to the trolley on which the old man lay.

'You are surely not thinking of hastening his end, for some foul purpose? The man is dying and will be at peace soon enough. I will not stand by and watch you commit murder.'

Walter put a hand on my arm. 'No, my friend, we are doctors in the business of saving life, not disposing of it.'

'You swear?'

'I swear.'

I turned to Rafe, who nodded.

'Then I have done you an injustice.'

'No matter. But I am puzzled as to why you should think either Rafe or myself likely to be common murderers.'

I did not know. I could not say that something about their manner had been troubling me sorely and that this urgent journey to the bowels of the hospital at the dead of night had thoroughly unnerved me.

'Nevertheless, I think I am entitled to some explanation of all this.'

'You are and before long you will be our witness and I swear to you that we plan nothing nefarious and nothing to endanger a life which is about to draw up to a peaceful end.'

Walter stepped forward and put his hand out to the man who lay there, breathing with more and more difficulty. The rattle in his throat was more pronounced and once or twice, the grimy fingers and hand twitched. Once the eyelids seemed about to open but then did not. The gas in Rafe's burners hissed and popped softly, otherwise the room was quite silent.

Had Walter and Rafe succumbed to some sort of madness? But what sort would grip two men together yet not also cause them to appear feverish and raving? Insanity is not infectious unless it comes about as the result of some rabies-like infection and they both seemed eminently well.

They could simply have been two doctors paying close attention to a patient for whom all hope had gone. What was I doing there, I as sane as any other, for all that I felt nervous and baffled? Walter had said that I was their witness but what was I witnessing? Only an old man dying.

In the next moment something happened, his raucous breathing changed, slowed and quietened.

'Now!' Walter said in an urgent tone and at once, Rafe crossed to the bench and took up a glass phial, a length of narrow tubing and a test-tube, together with what resembled an oxygen mask, but with a couple of alterations. He went up to the dying man and put the mask over his face. It sat loosely and he appeared quite unaware of it – indeed, I thought that the man was unaware of everything now. One end of the tubing was fixed to the mask and the other into the top of the phial and secured by a clip. The phial had two small holes in the side. Rafe held the test tube up and I saw some clear liquid, perhaps to a depth of half an inch, in the bottom. We were now all standing in such silence and stillness that our own breathing seemed to slow almost to a stop. There was no sound.

The old man's face was sunken in, the flesh already waxen. He breathed two more shallow breaths, then a third. I thought that I could hear the pounding not only of my own heart but that of Walter and Rafe's, too.

There came one more, unsteady breath and Walter said again 'Now!' But in a voice so faint that I barely heard him. On the same instant, Rafe poured the clear liquid out of the test tube into the phial. The old man exhaled for the last time and the breath travelled down from the mask over his face into the tubing. For a split second I saw it mist the inside of the glass. He breathed no more and at the very second that he was still, and in death, the liquid in the phial seemed to catch fire and to turn not into an ordinary flame but a sort of phosphorescent gas that crept up the inside of the glass, a very slightly pulsating substance, semi-transparent and astonishingly beautiful. I gazed at it in amazement and in disbelief. It remained when Rafe disconnected the tubing and quickly stopped the aperture. He held up the phial. I glanced at Walter and saw that he was transfixed by it and that his face wore an almost beatific expression – partly of triumph and partly what I can only call joy. Then he gave a small sigh and we all looked at the old man.

His chest did not rise. He was utterly still and his face was changed by a look of utter tranquillity. Walter bent and lifted each of his eyelids and then beckoned me to move closer. He handed me his ophthalmic torch and I bent to examine the corpse's pupils.

'Fixed and dilated,' I said.

'Pulse?'

I held first one wrist then the other, for a full minute and put my finger to the carotid artery. I took the stethoscope and listened closely to the chest. There was nothing – no breath, no heartbeat, no sign of life at all.

'To the best of my knowledge and observation, this man is dead.'

There was an almost reverential hush. Rafe stood on the other side of the trolley, holding the glass. The beautiful light contained within it gleamed silver white and still phosphorescent and as we stared at it we saw that it still pulsed faintly in time with the beating of our hearts.

'So – there we have it,' Walter said.

I managed to pull myself out of my half-trance.

'I suppose you call whatever is in that phial "the spark of life" and I presume you now have plans to replace it into the dead body and wait for a resurrection?' I shuddered. The room was deathly cold, though I had been quite unconscious of the fact until now. I was badly frightened and completely out of my depth medically, ethically and simply as a human being. Walter touched my arm and I jumped back. His eyes were still sparking with excitement but his voice was full of concern.

'No,' he said. 'This man, whoever he is, will now be left to rest in peace and accorded a proper burial, by the Christian church – for which, by the way, though not a member, I have a profound respect.'

'Close by,' Rafe said, still holding the phial, which continued to gleam and pulsate, 'is the hospital mortuary, to which our friend here will now be taken. And then we plan to conduct the next and most vital phase of our experiment. I am warning you now, you, as I have warned Walter many times, it is the part most is likely to fail, though I have a flicker of confidence, based on experiments I have already conducted in my laboratory.'

'The cat!'

'Indeed, but after all, one ginger cat may easily be confused with another and besides, the cat is a living organism but it is not a human being. It lacks many attributes of the human and many religious people would say that a cat has no soul.'

I felt giddy and put my hand to my head. 'Is this night never to end? Will there be no conclusion to the strange events?'

As I swayed, Walter took firm hold of me and held me, while letting me slide gently to the floor. He propped me up with my back against the wall and then pushed me forwards with my head between my knees.

'If you still feel unsteady in five minutes, I will take you home. You are a robust man but you were gravely ill at the end of last year and you have just been subjected to a severe nervous strain.'

'No,' I said, as the swirling sensation behind my eyes gradually slowed, like a fairground carousel coming to a standstill. 'No, I intend to see this through. I am your witness and I won't let you down.'

'Good man. Now drink this.' He held a small flask. 'No no, it is simply a good brandy, it will do you nothing but good. I intend to have a dram myself.'

I took a good mouthful and the liquid fire of it re-invigorated me in seconds. I stood up. Walter was ready with a hand but I did not need it.

'I am quite well,' I said, 'and quite ready.'

3

We covered the face and body of the old
vagrant with a sheet and Walter and Rafe
left the small room, Rafe pushing the
trolley, Walter walking a step or two ahead.
The corridors were empty and silent – any
sounds from the main body of the hospital did not penetrate this subterranean
annex. The old mortuary – there was a
much newer one in the East Wing – was
close by and unattended because it was
now little used, but because of the recent
influx of mortally ill patients, it was fully
equipped and functioning. Walter had a

key – I did not ask how he had obtained it.

'Is Rafe not coming with us?'

'We have things to attend to in readiness. You will stay here and guard our departed friend.' He glanced almost fondly at the sheeted body.

'Where are you going?'

'You seem nervous – surely you are accustomed to death by now?'

'I am agitated about what you and Rafe are doing. You must agree that it is hardly regular or normal.'

'It is unique,' Walter said.

'Perhaps, but as to remaining alone here with our friend – of course I am not nervous.'

'I am pleased to hear it,' Walter smiled and I realised what had always perturbed me about that smile. It was not sinister, though it was not especially pleasant but it had an odd effect. It changed his face from that of a young, fresh-faced man into one far older. It was uncanny. He was twenty-six but instantly became ancient, his features showing briefly the ravages of old age and bitter, even terrible experience. He glanced at me as he closed the mortuary door, leaving me alone and as the smile had faded his face was young again, the face on which few cares or troubles had made any mark. How peculiar, that the change should be wrought by a smile.

Being alone with a dead man did not perturb me in the least and I lifted the sheet to look again at his face. It still wore the expression of great calm and acceptance. I could discern, beneath the ravages of a hard lived life, and of ageing, that the man had once been handsome, with a broad brow and a well-shaped and resolute mouth. There was a gentleness about him which was delightful and strangely comforting. Whatever his life had been, death had resolved all suffering and troubles. I covered his face. No, I was not in the least afraid of a corpse which could do me no harm, but I was terrified of what living men might be about. The phrase 'playing with fire' came to mind, followed by remembrance of horrible stories, so that I was relieved when I heard the key being turned in the lock.

Rafe came in first, still carrying the glass phial, as if it contained a rare and precious oil. Walter was at his heels, pulling another trolley into the room, upon which another figure lay. He locked the door behind him.

'What –?'

He did not answer but stationed the trolley under the lamp.

'I need to call upon you again,' he said to me. 'You are my witness.'

He drew down the sheet and I caught my breath. The body was that of a young woman of eighteen or twenty years, wearing a green cotton hospital gown. Her hair was a rich brown, with the reddish tinge of a chestnut fresh from its carapace. Her skin was flawless. She was beautiful.

'Again,' Walter said at my side, 'as with our other body, we do not know her identity. She was brought into the hospital two days ago, found gravely ill with hypothermia on the river embankment. I attended to

her and saw at once that here was the other half of the equation – if that does not put it too crudely. We made strenuous efforts to save her but when it became clear that we would not do so, I called Rafe. When I arrived here with you earlier, I hastened to find our old man and ascertain how much longer he had to live.'

All three of us looked down at the young woman. She was still breathing in a shallow and faltering rhythm. Walter felt her pulse.

'Weak and very slow.' His voice dropped to a whisper so that I felt he was talking to himself. 'If only she knew. If only …'

'I hope you do not intend to do her any injury or harm. Leave her to slip away peacefully, for God's sake. Leave your shabby experiments at least to the old and hopeless.'

Walter simply shook his head and did not reply. All gazed silently at the dying girl. There was no harsh rattle this time, merely a few sounds in her throat, as if she was trying to cough. Walter turned urgently to Rafe, who held the phial containing the pulsating phosphorescence, and a fresh oxygen mask which he quickly attached to the girl's face.

'Careful – wait – be very careful,' Walter said urgently. My mouth was dry, my eyes staring so that I scarcely blinked.

On the instant and without further warning, the girl's breathing stopped and at once the shadow of death, invisible yet almost tangible, crept over her face.

'Now!'

A split second and Rafe had started to squeeze the tube attached by one end to the phial and the other to the girl's mouth beneath the mask. The liquid flared up and became radiant as it travelled at great speed out of the phial until the glass was empty. We all held our breath and then I felt as if the air in the whole room had somehow lightened and taken on a life of its own. I felt my heart leap, I felt jubilant, joyous, more alive than I had ever been. I felt newborn. When I looked at the others, I saw by a strange pearlescence on their skin and light in their eyes that they experienced it too. It all lasted only a thousandth of a second and yet it seemed to last for all eternity, and when it faded, I felt as if I had been let down from the air, to land softly, safely, on the ground by Rafe's side. I did not dare to think, speculate, hope. I let my mind go blank. My body seemed held together by the finest of wires, which was taut but quite painless. And then I looked down.

The girl was breathing. Her pallor had the faintest colouring as the blood re-filled arteries, veins, capillaries, just below the skin. Her fingernails were flushed pink. She did not open her eyes, her body did not stir. Walter passed me the stethoscope and I could feel the trembling in his hand. I bent over the now living girl and listened to her heartbeat, heard the sound of air passing in and out of her lungs. I felt her pulse and lifted each eyelid in turn. The pupils were bright but unseeing. She was not conscious but as I removed the stethoscope, I said, 'I have no doubt that she is alive.'

Walter grabbed Rafe's hand in a grip so tight that the man winced.

'You have succeeded!'

Rafe was deathly pale.

'You have raised the dead!'

'No!' I said, and was startled to hear how loud and emphatic my voice sounded in the quiet room. 'You go too far. Your claim is too immense – it is not credible. It defies everything I know, or I have been taught – it defies human experience.'

'Yes,' Walter said, 'it does indeed. But now we must be practical. The young woman must be taken back to an acute ward and put under close observation. I will take her myself and instruct the nursing staff. Rafe must attend to the dead man. We will meet again at Printer's Devil Court where my prescription is a glass each of good brandy.'

We watched Walter wheel away the still-breathing young woman. Our own work was quickly done. We left the old mortuary and locked the door. Rafe took possession of the key and we went, neither of us speaking, out of the hospital and up through the dark and deserted streets in the bitter cold, to our lodgings.

4

'One thing I do not understand and that is why? What possible reason could you have for performing this whole charade?'

We were all three of us sitting round the fire, which was smoking and sulking dismally in the grate, in spite of our best efforts. None of us was calm enough to sleep. I had said nothing on the way home or for some time after we had all our brandy and battled with the fire but I had been thinking hard, my brain trying to produce a plausible explanation for what had happened, which had shocked and un-nerved me until, as if some piece finally clicked into place, I saw what should have been clear all along. Walter and Rafe had performed an elaborately staged series of clever conjuring tricks.

'You went to a good deal of trouble,' I said now. 'You prepared the way carefully and prepared me too for that matter and at some considerable risk. I see it all but I still do not see a reason, so perhaps before we retire please, Walter and Rafe, an explanation.'

Then I saw that Walter was angry. His mouth was tight, his eyes narrowed.

'You do not understand – *you*? Correct me, Hugh, but I think we are the ones owed an explanation and an apology.'

'How so?'

'Do you not believe the evidence of your own eyes? How can what you witnessed tonight be some kind of trick or charade? If it had been then I agree you would be fully entitled to ask for a reason and an explanation, but credit us with more intelligence and maturity. What possible reason indeed could be behind such a trick? What a puerile game we would have been playing, what a waste of our time and energy – what an offence that would have been.'

'You cannot expect me to believe that it was anything other than a fraud.'

'I do expect it. What we witnessed was a triumphant success – the culmination of much work and strain over many months and many setbacks.'

I stood up. 'So you refuse to give me your reason – so be it. I am horrified that you should have played such macabre games with the bodies of your patients. Shame on you. I want no more part of it. I will find new lodgings. I bid you both good night and God grant you forgiveness which is better than you deserve.'

I did not go to bed, merely took off my jacket and shoes, loosened my collar and sat in my chair for the few hours that re-mained of the night, in a turmoil of con-fused and angry thoughts. I could not forget the sight of the old vagrant dying before us, and the look of release and acceptance on his face. I could not forget the sight of the beautiful young woman in her coma, in that cold basement room. I intended to scour the hospital on the following day, to find her and discover what state she was in and whether she was expected to recover. About Walter and Rafe I could do nothing. I had, of course, no evidence of their nefarious activities. I wanted nothing more to do with them and prayed that whatever the reason for their dark and secret games, they would now cease to dabble in them and let the dead and the dying alone.

I wish now that I had taken James's course. I could never *un*-know what I now knew or forget whatever it was that I had witnessed. James would be deeply troubled not the least because, in his eyes, they had spoken blasphemously in their casual talk of 'raising the dead' and even gone on to pretend that they had done so. I might almost have believed them, had the old man, who I had confidently pronounced dead, woken. He had not. He had remained dead. The young woman, of course, had never been dead at all.

Altogether, I was ashamed to have had the smallest part in it.

I felt unwell the next morning, weak and exhausted. I did not go into the hospital and on the day after that, being worse, I again took myself to Norfolk, where I became seriously ill, my nervous system shattered, and I spent many weeks recuperating. I suffered from appalling nightmares and waking terrors, so much so that our family physician questioned whether I was fit to return to the hospital and continue my medical career. This roused me, and I realised how badly my body, mind and spirits had been affected. But that was my turning point. I pulled myself up, determined to return to the practice of medicine.

A year later I left London for a hospital in the West Country. I worked hard, my interest and enthusiasm fully roused again and gradually, I forgot Walter, Rafe and all their sinister trickeries.

James wrote to me to say that he had abandoned medicine, to study for the Ministry. Of Walter and Rafe, I heard nothing.

children of our own
…ubled me. Both Elea-
…n up to be fine young
…into the army, Laurie
…ootsteps and I took a
…t and pleasure in ob-
…hrough medical school
…s a doctor. He had no
…physician in a country
…, as he put it, but went
…h, made a pioneering
…tic defects in children
…ntry's leading expert
…d treatment. He spent
…abroad. Earlier in the
…vrite, he had finally re-
…vn to see us. He was in
…en, the prime of life, a
…vith his mother's deep
…tness of temperament.
…three of us at dinner
…er his return and when
…t on the table, Laurie
…ne bottle of claret you
…. (He and Toby had

Part Three

did not produce an
but that had never t
nor's boys had grov
men. Toby had gon
had followed in my
great deal of intere
serving his progress
and into his career
desire to be a family
parish – bury himsel
into medical resear
study of certain gen
and became the co
in their diagnosis an
some time travelling
year of which I now
turned and came do
his late thirties by th
tall, handsome man
brown eyes and swe

We were only the
on that first night af
the beef had been s
said, 'That looks a
have opened, Hugh

never called me by anything other than my Christian name since childhood, in accordance with our wishes and out of respect for their late father.)

'Good enough for a toast.'

'It is indeed,' I said, touching the St Emilion from an especially fine year. 'Tell us what news you have that deserves toasting.'

Eleanor looked at her son, a slight flush coming to her cheeks. 'Are you going to be married, Laurie?'

He let out a shout of laughter. 'Whenever have I had the chance to look around for a wife? No, no, you will have to wait a long time before that happens. I have been appointed as consultant physician at St Luke's – your own hospital, Hugh!'

In the midst of the general rejoicing and congratulations, a sudden chill descended on me, so that I had to force myself to remain full of laughter and good spirits, but it passed before long. I was proud of Laurie and delighted for him but I never wanted to set foot in that hospital again. However, some six months after he had taken up his appointment, I was obliged to do so.

Laurie was presenting a paper to a learned medical society, a great honour, and of course I must attend. Eleanor was away on a visit to her aged mother so that I went up to London alone. Laurie booked me a room in St Luke's club – for past and present members of the hospital. It was well-appointed, the public rooms were delightfully comfortable, in an old-fashioned way and I went off to hear the lecture wondering why I did not come to London more often, country bumpkin that I had become.

After the event, we enjoyed a celebratory dinner and then, as Laurie wanted to stay up into the small hours talking to his colleagues, I left them to it. Just before midnight I set off to walk back to the club. My route was the old one, but this corner of London had changed a good deal. Fleet Street no longer housed the hot-metal presses and many of the old alleys and courts had long gone, most of them bombed to smithereens by the Blitz. Once or twice I took a wrong turn and ended up among new buildings I didn't recognise. At one point, I retraced my steps for a hundred yards and suddenly I was thrown back in time. I realised that the old Printers Devil's Court, where I had lodged, had been laid waste and that the hospital club was now sited on part of the same ground. I thought little of it – Printer's Devil Court held no special memories for me, other than those last peculiar and unpleasant ones.

I was about to turn into the club when I noticed that there was still a passageway to one side and saw the tower of St-Luke's-at-the-Gate rising up ahead of me in the fitful moonlight. I stood stock still. London churches are always a fine sight and I was glad that this one, with a surprising number of others, had escaped destruction. The passageway ended at the back of the old graveyard, as before, and that seemed unchanged, the tombstones still leaning this way and that and even more thickly covered in moss.

And then I saw her. She was a few yards

away from me, moving among the graves, pausing here and there to bend over and peer, as if trying to make out the inscriptions, before moving on again. She wore a garment of a pale silvery grey that seemed strangely gauze-like and her long hair was loose and free. She had her back to me. I was troubled to see a young woman wandering here at this time of night and started towards her, to offer to escort her away. She must have heard me because she turned and I was startled by her beauty, her pallor and even more, by the expression of distress on her face. She came towards me quickly, holding out her hand and seeming about to plead with me, but as she drew near, I noticed a curious blank and glassy look in her eyes and a coldness increased around me, more intense than that of the night alone. I waited. The nearer she came the greater the cold but I did not – why should I? link it in any way to the young woman, but simply to the effects of standing still in this place where sunlight rarely penetrated in which had a dankness that came from the very stones and from the cold ground.

'Are you unwell?' I asked. 'You should not be here alone at this time of night – let me see you safely to your home.'

She appeared puzzled by my voice and her body trembled beneath the pale clothes.

'You will catch your death of cold.'

She stretched out both her hands to me then but I shrank back, unaccountably loathe to take them. Her eyes had the same staring and yet vacant look now that she was close to me. But she was fully alive and breathing and I had no reason to fear.

'Please tell me what is wrong?'

There was a second only during which we both stood facing one another silently in that bleak and deserted place and something seemed to happen to the passing of time, which was now frozen still, now hurtling backwards, now propelling us into the present again, but then on, and forwards, faster and faster, so that the ground appeared to shift beneath my feet, yet nothing moved and when the church clock struck, it was only half past midnight.

'Please help me. I need someone to help me.'

I would have replied again to ask her how I could help but I was silenced, not by her words, but by her voice, which was not that of a girl of no more than eighteen or twenty, but of an old man, a deep, hoarse voice, cracked and wavering. It was like hearing a puppet-master accidentally speaking in the voice of one doll while pulling the strings of another. I recoiled but I also went on staring at the girl not only because of the voice but because now I knew that I had seen her before – in the basement room of the hospital some forty years earlier, lying on a trolley and subject to the vile tricks played by Walter and Rafe.'

'Sir? I have been searching for so long. Please help me.'

She was walking away from me and now began to move in and out between the graves again, going to first one and then another, quickening her pace, faster and faster, so that she seemed to be floating just above the ground. At each stone she bent and peered briefly at the inscription, though most of them were so overgrown and worn away by the weather, that few were legible. I followed her every step. I could not help myself. But at each grave, she let out a low, harsh cry of disappointment.

'Tell me,' I said, 'I will try to help you. Are you looking for a particular grave? That of a parent perhaps? A loved one? Let us look together, though we had really better do it in the daylight.'

She sank to the ground then and bent her head. 'My own …' she said.

'Your own family? Or perhaps even your own child?'

She shook her head violently, as if she was angry that I did not understand.

'Taken …' She seemed to have greater difficulty in forming the words now, as if she had little breath left and her voice sounded even older.

'The … wrong … life …'

My blood felt as if it flowed more and more slowly through my veins and I felt the chill tighten around me again. I looked in horror at the young woman and as I did so, one moment she was there, kneeling on the cold ground trying desperately to speak, and the next, she seemed to be dissolving, to become absorbed, like the damp, into the rough earth in front of the grave. I closed my eyes in terror of what I was seeing and when I opened them again she had gone. She was simply no longer there before me. Nothing was there. Nothing at all.

Seconds later, I seem to be dissolving too and then the stones around me and the walls of the church, all seemed to shimmer and fade and then go black.

I surfaced from a swirl of nightmares to find Laurie bending over me and as his features materialised from the mist, I realise that I was in my bed at the club. He told me that he and some fellows had taken a short cut home from their evening at the hospital dinner and found me lying insensible. Having checked that I was not injured but had merely fainted, they had carried me back between them.

I recovered quickly, my head cleared and after drinking some brandy and hot water, I sat beside the fire. It was then that I told the whole story to Laurie, from the events in my days at the hospital and Printer's Devil Court. When I reached the climax of the tale, with Rafe transferring the contents of the phial to the dead young woman, Laurie started up.

'Walter Powell! That name is known in the medical world – though I know you never hear a word of these things, buried as you are in the country. His name is known and so is that of his cohort, Rafe McAllister. They were apprehended in the course of stealing a body from the mortuary at St Luke's and from taking away a patient who was on the point of death, without permission or authority. A night porter gave testimony and one of his fellows swore to having seen the two men about their dreadful business more than once. He had alerted the hospital authorities but nothing was done. In fact, that porter was dismissed – I dare say he was believed to have had a breakdown. Nothing more was reported for over a year, when the two men were caught and police were called. I only know all this from hospital legend and reading up old newspapers. A macabre and distasteful business and quite inexplicable. I was mildly interested. I like to study peculiarities of human behaviour, as you know, but I came to the conclusion that it must all have been some money-making lark – that or blackmail though God knows how or what. The days of Burke and Hare are long gone.'

'Did you hear what happened to the two men? Presumably they went to jail.'

'I have no idea – I gave up reading about it – I'm far too busy. I know they were given bail on the usual conditions, that they surrender their passports and reported to the police but more than that ...' Laurie held out his hands.

'Meanwhile, Hugh, you are obviously sickening for something. Whatever caused you to pass out must be investigated – I am having you in St Luke's first thing tomorrow.'

It was clear that he had not taken my story seriously but put it down to the ravings of a man with a feverish illness of some kind. But I knew that the scene was no delusion. It was as real as the furniture in that club bedroom.

'I have no need of any hospitalisation, thank you Laurie. I am tired and a little chilled. A good night's sleep will sort that out and I will be right as rain tomorrow. I will return to my quiet, dull ways in the depths of the country, where no ghost has ever troubled me.'

He knew that I meant what I said and got up to leave it, but at the door he turned.

'I do not believe in ghosts,' he said, 'nor in the raising of the dead to life.'

'No. Until tonight, nor did I.'

He sighed and left, saying that he would check on me in the morning before he would countenance my going home.

As soon as he had gone, I felt restless and anxious, not for myself but for the young woman, whatever – *whatever* she was. She had asked me for help. Did she linger about the churchyard night after night searching and pleading?

I dressed and went downstairs. The night porter's cubby-hole had a low light showing within and the man was leaning back in his leather armchair, eyes closed, snoring gently, but as soon as I started to creep towards the outer door, he woke.

'Are you well, sir? What can I do for you?'

'I need to take a turn in the air. Would you be so kind as to let me out?' He looked perturbed.

'I should not be gone long but I find this is usually the way to settle myself if I am restless.'

He unlocked a side door to the main entrance and told me it would be open and he himself awake, on my return.

'Don't stay out too long, Sir, or hang about the back streets – you never know, at this hour.'

I knew that I would see her. She was wondering anxiously among the graves, just as before, leaning down to read the inscriptions. I make no sound but she turned, as if sensing my presence. Her expression was lost, distraught and she lifted her arm up.

'Help me. I cannot find … Find …'

The voice was old, as before, that of an old man. It was still so very strange and unnerving but I forced myself to remain calm.

'What are you looking for? You know that if I can help you I will.' She covered her eyes with her hands.

'Don't be afraid of me.' She said nothing.

'Tell me again.'

'I have … I am … Nothing.'

'What are you looking for?'

'I am … Not. I have … Not.' She gave a long and weary sigh and her whole body shuddered. 'The wrong life.' The words came out after a great effort. 'Help me … I must … Must … Find.'

What those two men had tried to do was not possible, and it was madness, terrifying and unimaginable, but that their terrible experiment had somehow succeeded in part I could not now doubt. The life force they had captured and transfused was no mere anonymous breath or spark, it was imprinted with the character – the being – the soul even – of the dead man. Was this young woman still alive or had she died a second time and this for good? Had she been unable to rest, or move on until she was rid of 'the wrong life' and re-united with her true self? Was she a ghost? But she spoke. Does a ghost speak? How could I know?

The next moment, again, she was no longer there. Had she slipped away, out of the side gate? Gone into the church perhaps? But I would have seen her, sensed some movement. She had not passed me. The moon was behind clouds, it was pitch dark but my eyes were so well adjusted to it that I could make out the graves, the wall, the church tower. I waited. I called out but my voice sounded oddly hollow and unreal, fading into the emptiness.

The next morning, I told Laurie I had

changed my mind and wanted to stay another night. I needed to look up a few bits of information in the hospital records.

I found everything. The old man was listed as Patient A207. He had been certified dead by Walter Powell M.D. Touchingly, although I learned that the A stood for Anonymous, he had been given a burial name – John.

A young woman, Patient A194, was recorded a couple of days earlier, having been picked up from the street in an unconscious state. A locket had been found on her person with the name Grace barely visible on it. But there was no record of her death until several years later when again she had been found out of doors, suffering from malnutrition and hypothermia. The death certificate had been signed by a P. R. Ross M.D. but there was a pathologist's report inserted – a post-mortem had been requested by the coroner, as was by then becoming usual for those found dead on the streets of London. The body was that of a young woman aged around twenty-five to twenty-eight. She was severely malnourished, but this would not have accounted for her having the vocal cords, larynx and lungs of someone over seventy years, who had been a heavy tobacco smoker. 'Inconsistent with other findings' was jotted to one side in the usual pathologist's barely legible hand.

I closed the record book with a strange feeling of relief. I had to find one further piece of information and then I would have all I needed to bring the whole business to a conclusion. If I was insane, hallucinating or suffering the effects of a brain injury, then I had no symptoms. I had a clear head, a calm mind, a steady pulse and a resolution as firm as I had ever known.

I did not mention any of it to Lauric. We ate supper together, during which he was full of medical talk. He glanced at me sharply once or twice, but I thought that everything about my demeanour and easy conversation put him at ease. When I told him that I was to travel home the next day on the late morning train I saw the relief in his eyes and I understood it fully. How could he possibly have believed my story? He was, like me, a doctor and a scientist and he knew far more than I did about delusional states. Although the boundaries of what was possible in medicine had been pushed farther than I would have ever thought possible as a young doctor, they surely could never extend to raising the dead. If what Walter and Rafe had done was real, we had better throw away all our textbooks and templates and prior assumptions, for the very ground on which we stood was unstable. Whatever the truth, whatever I had seen, I knew I must make a last attempt to lay it all to rest. If I did not, I feared I would never sleep again.

Just after 1 o'clock in cold clear moonlight I was waiting for her again, and again she seemed to materialise on an instant and was wandering among the graves as before. When she looked up and saw me, she beckoned. She wore the same thin grey clothes, her feet were bare and her flesh had a faint blue sheen.

'Help me – please help me.'

'I can and I will,' I said, going over to her, 'but this is not the place. You must follow me.'

The old churchyard led, through an opening in the far wall, to a more recent burial ground, with some twenty identical gravestones, little worn or touched by the moss and lichen. I had discovered that the hospital had taken over the space for the burials of patients whose identities were unknown of whom there used to be many more than there are now. I led the way to two of the graves, marked simply John and Grace above a date and a simple cross.

She was standing beside the entrance and I beckoned to her. She said again 'Help me, please help me,' in that old, croaking voice, her eyes vacant. I still shuddered to hear it as I looked at her beautiful face. Then, with steps that seemed hardly to touch the ground, she came close to me and as she did so, and for the first time, I smelled the smell of death and decay upon her. I did not shrink back. She approached the grave marked John and at once recoiled. I edged closer, speaking to her as reassuringly as I would to a child. I thought that I now understood what was wrong, though I was working more or less on blind instinct and I had a notion of how she might find her rest and resolution at last. She turned to me, looking fearful.

'No,' I said, speaking in as quiet and reassuring voice as I could. 'There is nothing for you to be frightened of. In this grave is the body of the old man whose life you were given. I can explain it no more clearly – it is beyond my understanding.'

She bent to read the inscription and I saw her whole being begin to tremble as she reached out her hand, as if to trace the outline of the lettering. I moved slowly along to the grave marked Grace and stopped beside it and as I did so I felt that same deathly chill wrap me round. She was standing very close to me and it seemed as if her breath was becoming fainter. The cold grew more intense. I was afraid myself now and felt unreal, as if I was standing beside my own body but I managed to speak, though it was hard and I could only get out a few words. 'Grace. Find. Go.' My chest seemed to be tightening and my throat about to close up.

'Back. Give. Back.' I could say no more. My brain was working slowly, in flashes of consciousness between terrible stretches of darkness. I knew what she must do, and that I was trying to help her as she had begged me. She took a couple of steps forwards. I did not see her turn again and now she was beside John's grave. I stared. Nothing happened and the bitter cold was binding me with iron bands now and the constriction in my chest was agonisingly painful. She glanced once more at her 'own' grave and I saw intense suffering and distress in her face, before she took a single further step, so that now she was standing right on the burial place. And then she had gone. She was no longer there. Nothing was there. At once, the chill that had held me lifted, and the pain and constriction were loosed.

I came to, as if I had woken from sleep but not from any dreams. I was fully conscious of where I was and of everything that had happened. Whatever help Grace had needed, I felt sure I had given it to her but I could do no more and I made my way towards the passage. The clouds had almost cleared and the moon shone with a soft hazy light. I looked back. Above the grave of John was a pale mist, not visible in any other part of the churchyard. It had no form and there was no sense of 'presence'. It was like the mist that sometimes happens over the surface of water at dawn. As I looked, it began to dissolve and I felt an uneasy calm. Whatever I had done, whatever had happened, I believed that the young woman had now found her peace, and that both she and the old man were somehow whole and restored.

Part Three

5

I travelled to London rarely. In the past twenty years, I had visited no more than half a dozen times. I had a horror of the place and I had never again ventured to my old hospital nor set foot near Fleet Street and its environs. Many people enjoy revisiting old haunts but a shadow fell on me if I so much as thought about them.

I practised as a country physician in a most beautiful and peaceful part of England for almost forty years and married a young widow, Eleanor Barnes, who brought me a fine brace of stepsons. We did not produce any children of our own but that had never troubled me. Both Eleanor's boys had grown up to be fine young men. Toby had gone into the army, Laurie had followed in my footsteps and I took a great deal of interest and pleasure in observing his progress through medical school and into his career as a doctor. He had no desire to be a family physician in a country parish – bury himself, as he put it, but went into medical research, made a pioneering study of certain genetic defects in children and became the country's leading expert in their diagnosis and treatment. He spent some time travelling abroad. Earlier in the year of which I now write, he had finally returned and came down to see us. He was in his late thirties by then, the prime of life, a tall, handsome man with his mother's deep brown eyes and sweetness of temperament.

We were only the three of us at dinner on that first night after his return and when the beef had been set on the table, Laurie said, 'That looks a fine bottle of claret you have opened, Hugh. (He and Toby had

6

At home, work and country life absorbed me again and although I cannot pretend that I forgot about what had happened or that my sleep was always untroubled, on the whole I was fairly at ease.

A year passed. We saw a Laurie infrequently – he was rarely free from the hospital – and when we did meet, he and I never referred to what I had told him.

One bright, clear morning in October, I opened a letter addressed to me alone, in Laurie's hand, which was somewhat surprising but I told Eleanor I had been expecting some medical information from him and, because I had a sense of foreboding, I delayed opening it until I was alone.

My dear Hugh,

In haste, but I thought this might interest you. The names caught my eye in the paper and remembering your strange stories, I looked at the records for the era at St Luke's of those two doctors you knew. As you remember, Powell and McAllister were arrested, charged and bailed on various dreadful suspicions. They were both dismissed from the hospital and subsequently struck off the medical register 'for behaviour in a manner so as to call the profession into disrepute'.

They were accused of gross misconduct in relation to the certification and preparation of deceased patients and the improper disposal of their remains but there must have been far more to it, none of which could be proved.

I confess that I doubted your tale until I came upon this and of course, I am sure you are not surprised to hear that I still believe parts of it to be entirely fanciful – you could never resist embellishing a good story, as I recall from boyhood! I wondered what had happened to Powell and McAllister – who I assumed must have been imprisoned for some years but later released. Such men often disappear abroad, where they do not find it as difficult as it should be to continue practising medicine. I asked frequently if any older members of the hospital medical staff recalled them and eventually an eminent pathologist, sometime retired, raised an eyebrow and said that such things were best forgotten but then he added, 'Their bodies were washed up just a few days after they were released on bail. I performed the post mortems. As I recall, both of the stomachs were full of strychnine and their hands and arms were held together by chains.' I asked if he had suspected murder.

'Who knows? But for my money it was a clear case of joint suicide. They were unable to live with themselves any longer and the world was well rid of them.'

The case may not be closed in police files but I am inclined to take the pathologist's view. So there you have it – a melancholy little tale but I hope you're interested to hear the end of it.

I had always known that what Walter and Rafe were dabbling in was evil and dangerous and there was no doubt in my mind now that the pathologist was correct. They had taken their own lives out of shame, guilt and terror of what they had done. It would have led to worse. They had stopped themselves in the only certain way. I felt nothing but cold contempt for them. I like to think that I am a compassionate man but in this, my heart was hard.

5

Postscript

Here, the small book ends. When eventually I read it, after my stepfather's death, I presumed that there was no more to be added. Whatever the truth of his story that was it —'a story'. Many a writer has told a tale in the first person and his own voice, as if he is recounting real events but I was entertained by the way Hugh had done it, presumably as a diversion from the often humdrum life of a country doctor. Why he had chosen this particular topic on which to base his fiction I had no idea but it was as good as many others and makes for a creepy tale.

At least, that was what I thought when I received the little book. I read it, put it away on the shelf and forgot all about it.

Hugh died at the age of ninety-two, pretty well and in command of his faculties until almost the end, when he became confused and not always fully aware of us or his surroundings. I thought he had suffered a small stroke, though if so, it did not cause him any physical problems and he continued to read and write letters to old colleagues, to play chess, do *The Times* crossword and to enjoy visits from Toby and myself. Toby, having retired from the Army and married, bought a small farm only half an hour from Hugh and Eleanor. I continued to work in London at St Luke's, but I drove down to the country every other weekend, now that my parents were becoming increasingly frail.

My mother died a year before Hugh and of course, not only did he miss her greatly but he seemed to have a strong sense that he was nearing his own end. He stayed in the old house tended by two wonderful women from the village and the visiting nurse and I then went down every week. Toby or Joy, his wife and their two daughters, visited almost every day. I think that Hugh was as content as he could be and always seemed sanguine and philosophical and quite often downright cheerful.

He still took a daily walk around the village and even a little further afield when the weather was mild. He was well known and loved over a wide area, and often met with old patients and their descendants on his walks. They would stop their cars for a chat and frequently give him a lift home.

I was due to go down as usual for the weekend when, very late on a Thursday evening, I received an urgent phone call from Toby to tell me that Hugh was extremely ill. Mrs Barford had popped in to see him at half past three and he said he proposed going out for a last walk. It was early October, the sun had been shining all day and there was as yet no hint of winter frosts or chill winds. She had reminded him that it was dark by five now and that she would have his supper ready, as usual, for seven o'clock. She last saw him making his way across the garden, and through the gate which led to the orchard – a favourite walk of his. From the orchard, the path led to the church and he could then return home via the body of the village, in a circular walk.

He had not returned after well over an hour and by then it was quite dark. Mrs Barford had raised the alarm and within a few minutes several men from the village had formed a search party.

Hugh was found in the churchyard, lying on the grass among the older gravestones. It was clear that he had suffered a severe stroke. He was got home, the local doctor – Hugh had appointed him as his successor – had said that he was unlikely to live very much longer and might well suffer a second and fatal vascular incident at any time. He was to be kept at home and made comfortable – the hospital was twenty miles away and would be able to do nothing more for him. It would be a cruelty to take him there.

When I arrived, Hugh was semi-conscious, the left side of his face slightly contorted, which gave him a staring, vacant look, and I thought that he had been frightened. I imagine he felt the first symptoms and knew he was alone and might die out there. He could not speak and I sat with him, alternating with Toby, through that night. He drifted in and out of sleep and his expression did not change until just around dawn, when he struggled to sit up. I tried to settle him back comfortably again but he clawed at my hand and arm and I saw that there was a beseeching look in his eyes. His mouth moving, a few inarticulate sounds came, gravelly and hoarse, but he was not able to form any words. I tried asking him to press my hand if he wanted a drink or was in any pain but he only clawed again, several times, each time more weakly, his eyes intent on my face, as if asking, asking.

But asking what? It was more than distressing to be unable to understand or to help him and I felt only a great relief when, just after six o'clock in the morning, he gave a sigh, his face changed, flickered with something I can only describe as delight for a second and then his body relaxed and he breathed his last, quiet breath.

We had already decided to sell the house. Toby was very well settled as he was, and I did not have occasion to take it over – my life and work will always be in London. We disposed of the everyday contents but we went through all the objects of value, the pictures and books, dividing them between us and sending the remainder to a sale-room. Toby entrusted me with the task of going through Hugh's papers, most of which related to his lifetime as a doctor, and it was while doing so that I came upon the pages that follow, which I presume he had intended to form the last part of his book. They were written in Hugh's own hand, legible but wavering – indeed, towards the end the writing became a wild scrawl which confirmed to me that he had suffered from more than one stroke.

I found myself greatly upset and unnerved by what I read and I could not – cannot – take it easily or lightly, as I once could the original story. I cannot get them out of my mind. I cannot sleep for asking myself endless questions relating to the whole business, from its very beginning in the old lodgings in Printer's Devil's Court. Without knowing about the subsequent events, about Hugh's last walk to the churchyard at dusk and then his final hours, and the fear I saw on his face during his last moments I would still have taken it all as a tale he had cooked up himself. But as I read the ending over and over again, I became racked with doubts, troubled in my mind, unable to resolve any of it to my satisfaction. I still cannot.

I am horribly afraid that I never will.

Hugh's Final Pages

I had long forgotten all about her. But perhaps nothing is ever truly forgotten, it simply lies dormant, waiting to be re-awakened. Certainly I had not thought of her – of any of it – for many years when I took my walk through our churchyard that late evening. It is a beautiful spot, bordering orchards and meadows, and the gentle hills beyond. This was the soft end to a mellow autumn day. In a couple of weeks it would be Harvest Festival, the service I have always tried to attend. It means a great deal to us in the country. So I was in a calm and unruffled mood when I unlatched the wooden gate. Eleanor is buried here. I do not hang about her grave in a melancholy way, but I like to visit from time to time, to talk to her, to remember. I have never felt the least troubled or afraid in this sacred place. Why would I?

I turned and I saw her. There was no mistaking the young woman and I knew her at once. Everything raced in towards me as an incoming tide. I had thought her to be at rest. I had thought I had done all I could to ensure it. But now here she was and I was not only struck as if by lightning with the shock of seeing her, I was also confused. Why was she here? How did she find me? Seeing me, she stretched out both her arms and I saw the old, distraught and beseeching expression in her eyes, on her face. I felt unsteady but I also felt a sense of dread. I did not want to see her here, I did not want to remember.

'Go. Please go,' I managed to say. 'Go back. You do not belong here. You are not welcome. Leave me in peace. Go home.'

But she came quickly across the grass,

barely touching the ground, as before, still holding out her hands to me, pleading, 'I can do no more for you,' I said.

She stopped a few yards away from me and began to speak – or at least, she opened her mouth, her lips moved, framing a rush of desperate words. But no sound came. No sound at all. She went on and on, gesturing to me, touching her face, her mouth, showing me what I already understood. She was dumb. She had given the old man's voice back to him but she had never found her own again and she had been searching for it, and for me, all these years.

I began to shake violently and I fled from her, stumbled away, making as quickly as I could for the gate and my own orchard.

I looked back once, hoping not to see her but she was still there, as clear as day and now she seemed to have a faint glow of phosphorescence round her. She was still holding out her hands, pleading, pleading and I could not bear it. I did not know how, but then I knew I must try and help her, as I had helped her before and I stopped and called out, 'I will come back. I will come back.' And I will go, I will go back …

(Here, the writing peters out.)